POLAR POLKA

COUNTING POLAR BEARS IN ALASKA

Chérie B. Stihler

PAWS IV published by
SASQUATCH BOOKS

ILLUSTRATIONS BY Erik Brooks

Chérie's dedication:

To Polar Bears International, Fiona & All who look after our polar bears—Thank You!

Scott ~ "Olives"

Erik's dedication:

For Nanook, and 450ppm

Printed in China
Published by Sasquatch Books
Distributed by PGW/Perseus
15 14 13 12 11 10 09 08   10 9 8 7 6 5 4 3 2 1

Library of Congress Cataloging-in-Publication data is available.
ISBN-10: 1-57061-520-9
ISBN-13: 978-1-57061-520-7

Book design: Rosebud Eustace
More about the author at www.cheriestihler.com
More about the illustrator at www.erikbrooks.com

Sasquatch Books
119 South Main Street, Suite 400
Seattle, WA 98104
(206) 467-4300
www.sasquatchbooks.com
custserv@sasquatchbooks.com

10 polar bears with shaggy white fur played the **POLAR POLKA** on a bobbing iceberg.

A piece broke. A bear floated away.
Snowy owls FLAPpED in and decided to stay.

9 polar bears with shaggy white fur played the **POLAR POLKA** on a bobbing iceberg.

POP!

A piece broke. A bear floated away.
Arctic fox **JUMPED** over and started to play.

8 polar bears with shaggy white fur
played the **POLAR POLKA** on a bobbing iceberg.

Crack!

A piece broke. A bear floated away.
The northern lights DANCED with a swing and a sway.

7 polar bears with shaggy white fur
played the **POLAR POLKA** on a bobbing iceberg.

Crash!

A piece broke. A bear floated away.
Ravens SWOOpED down to add to the fray.

6 polar bears with shaggy white fur
played the POLAR POLKA on a bobbing iceberg.

BoiNK!

A piece broke. A bear floated away.
Seals and hares joined the BOOGIE.

More friends—hooray!

5 polar bears with shaggy white fur
played the **POLAR POLKA** on a bobbing iceberg.

WHOMP!

A piece broke. A bear floated away.
Musk ox pulled in after **SAILing** the bay.

4 polar bears with shaggy white fur
played the **POLAR POLKA** on a bobbing iceberg.

BINK!

A piece broke. A bear floated away.
The wolves played a **WILD** round of ice-cube croquet.

3 polar bears with shaggy white fur
played the **POLAR POLKA** on a bobbing iceberg.

PLOP!

A piece broke. A bear floated away.
Walrus served lunch and iced tea on a tray.

2 polar bears with shaggy white fur played the **POLAR POLKA** on a bobbing iceberg.

A piece broke. A bear floated away.
Whales jumped and WIGGLED in a water ballet.

SPLOOSH!!

1 polar bear with shaggy white fur
played the **POLAR POLKA** on a *crowded* iceberg.

...and then there were none.

O polar bears with shaggy white fur played the **POLAR POLKA** on a *sinking* iceberg.

Ker -

10 polar bears with shaggy white fur
pushed back all the pieces of the BROKEN iceberg.

They climbed back on to put things right,
and rocked the POLAR POLKA all winter's night!

Paws for Thought: An Author's Note

Plight of the Polar Bears

Polar bears are in trouble. Wild polar bears live **only** in the Arctic. They use Arctic sea ice to hunt for food. Pollution and greenhouse gases from things like cars speed up global warming. This melts the sea ice. In some places the sea ice has disappeared completely. With less sea ice, polar bears have trouble finding the food they need for themselves and their families. If current levels of greenhouse gases continue and global warming does not stop, Arctic sea ice will melt and not return. Polar bears would then have no more sea ice—but you can **help** reduce pollution and the greenhouse gases that result from it.

Easy Ways YOU Can Help!

Walk, ride your bike, and take the bus as often as you can. Cars puff out *carbon dioxide*, a greenhouse gas. Fewer cars on the road mean less pollution.

Save energy. That reduces greenhouse gases too. Hang your clothes on a clothesline or drying rack instead of using the dryer. Put on a sweater instead of turning up the heat. Turn off things that use electricity. Read books instead!

Take a shower. Baths use about 15–25 gallons (57–95 liters) of hot water. Showers use less hot water and that saves more energy.

Recycle your paper, plastics, aluminum, and glass at home and at school. Recycling is another way to save energy and reduce greenhouse gases.

Plant trees. Trees pull in *carbon dioxide*. They fight global warming and make clean air for us to breathe. Trees must be cut down to make new paper. More pollution happens. Use products made with recycled paper—save trees!

Ask your big people to shop with companies that do things like replant forests, save energy, and recycle. This is called reducing your ecological footprint on our Earth.

Write letters to people in your government. Let them know you care about polar bears. Ask them to share what they are doing to fight global warming and help the polar bears.